BUFFALO DREAMS

KIM DONER

WESTWINDS PRESS™

AUTHOR NOTE

At the core of any human group lives Story, the why and how of existence. For a culture to thrive, Story must be breathed into the mouths of the next generation and ever passed on. When guests listen, a tale is adopted then adapted, and becomes their Story, too.

The ancient legend of White Buffalo Calf Woman has been shared in different ways by many tribes, but the central belief remains the same: a helpful spirit becomes a white buffalo, heralding the return of prosperity to her people, where needs are met and hopes fulfilled. The chances of a white buffalo being born are one in ten million; when this event actually occurred in August of 1994, she was named Miracle.

Since her birth, well over 100,000 people have visited Miracle at the ranch of Dave and Valerie Heider. Most are of Native American descent; many have driven hundreds of miles simply to be in the presence of the white buffalo. Visitors often leave deeply personal gifts of greeting, and the gates of the ranch look like a shrine.

Inspired by remembered legends, a stirring news story, and the charming face of a white buffalo calf, I began this book. The models I used are Native Americans; the gifts left for the calf in the book bear authentic patterns, designs, and colors found in the art of not only the Sioux, but the Kiowa, Potawatomi, Cheyenne, Arapaho, Cherokee, Osage, and Ojibway—a wide variety of tribes. Last but not least, my home was recently graced by a visit from a very tame young buffalo. Buffy was the perfect lady for her stay, happy to roam my house with the lure of endless vanilla wafers.

As for dreamcatchers, they are a powerful example of how Story grows universally. Originated in Native America, dreamcatchers are now found worldwide, and their owners add meaningful touches to make each one unique. To give a dreamcatcher as a gift indicates your wish for someone to sleep well—but even more, it shows the desire that only good dreams find the dreamer.

And remember, magic doesn't make you do something special; when you do something special, it makes magic.

A legend lived.

Sarah Bearpaw sat glued to the television. The news went on: a buffalo calf had been born, the only white one in the world . . . straight out of a story shared by many tribes . . . the sign of good things to come. . . .

She watched the camera zoom into a barnyard. A small, snowy calf stood against the giant background of a mother buffalo. Sarah knew the old tale by heart, but she never thought it would come true.

A beautiful spirit named White Buffalo Calf Woman came to a dying tribe. She gave them a sacred pipe and said its smoke would carry their dreams up to the heavens, where she would hear them and answer. As she left their camp, she rolled on the ground and stood as a black buffalo. Three more times she rolled, and each time she changed color, from black to brown, to red, and to white.

They smoked her pipe and slept. She heard their dreams and answered. The next day, when the tribe awoke, their village was surrounded by a herd of buffalo. They were never hungry or cold again.

And now, she had returned in the form of this white calf.

Joe bounded in, followed by Daddy. "Sarah, guess what!" he said. "A white buffalo got borned, and we're gonna take a trip to see her! She's magic! At Grandpa's, we watched it on TV. Greg Little Wolf said touching a white buffalo is big medicine. So we're gonna take presents and . . ."

"Son, hold on." Daddy's voice was firm. "We'll take gifts to honor the white calf, but a buffalo is not for petting. We'll be lucky just to see her. Sarah, your mama can take off work. Joe will miss a few days of kindergarten. But what about your pow wow? When's that?"

"Not for two weeks. But by then, my dreamcatcher will be ready to display there. See?"

The dreamcatcher Sarah had since she was a baby looked very different now. A gift when she was born twelve years ago, it had hung above her crib to sift out bad dreams and let only good ones through. As she got older, Sarah tied bits and pieces of her memories to it, like charms on a bracelet. Heavy with wishes and full of hopes, it hung wherever she slept.

The children watched as their father reached into his vest and handed something to Sarah. "I brought you an eagle feather from Grandpa's old headdress," he said. "The bird that flies closest to heaven will give your dreams strength."

Joe said, "Daddy, I want one, too! Where's mine?"

"Son, this is for Sarah. As your dreams grow, your turn will come. But, hey, don't you need to pack for the trip? We're leaving right away. What about your sleeping bag? Where's your flashlight?"

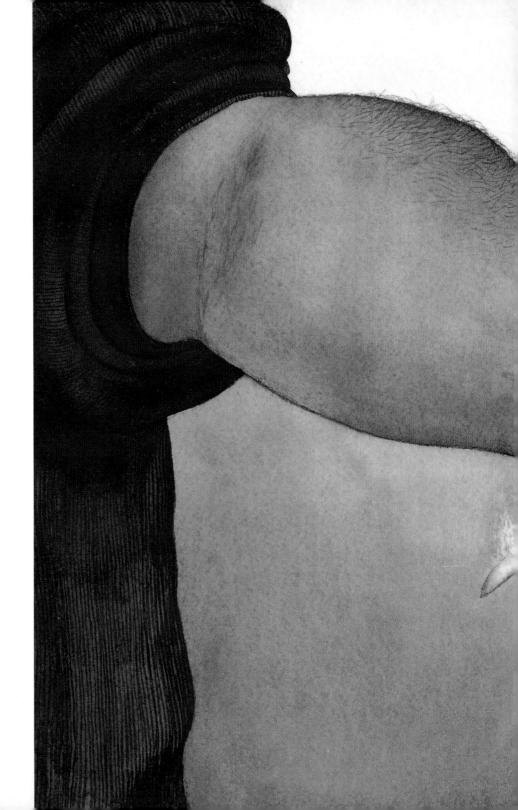

Joe was digging through his room when Mama got home from work. "Let's pack up that old camper and go!" she said.

Joe beamed his flashlight on her. She grabbed him and said, "What are you going to give the white calf, huh?" Mama smooched thick, wet kisses on his neck while Joe squirmed and giggled helplessly. "Little boy laughs? Little guy giggles?"

Sarah said, "I think I"ll give the eagle feather as my present, if that's okay." Her parents looked up. "I really wanted to hang it from my dreamcatcher, but, well . . ." she searched for the words, "the white calf is so tiny right now. I want her to have something strong, so her dreams can grow, too. Like mine!"

"To give strength to something other than yourself has its own rewards, Sarah," Daddy replied. "The feather belongs to you. You decide."

Soon the old camper hummed along as Daddy's harmonica blew tunes into the breeze. Sarah watched for cloud animals and thought about their trip. Daddy had said there was a giant tree in the barnyard where the buffalo lived. It bloomed with gifts from the people of many tribes. Tomorrow, bright and early, the Bearpaws would hang their gifts from the tree.

They arrived at the campground near the ranch where the white baby buffalo lived, and set up camp.

Joe galloped through the campground as Sarah looked for a place to hang her dreamcatcher for the night. She stopped a moment, and wondered.

What would be a good dream for a baby buffalo? Maybe . . . sweet grass, open fields, sunshine?

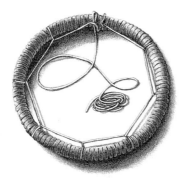

They were just about to settle into their sleeping bags when Mama pointed over the trees. The top of a barn could be seen, not too far away. "Oooooh, that must be where the white buffalo lives!" she said.

Joe stretched to see. He was very excited. "Daddy," he said, "she's a magic buffalo! I wanna touch her so I'll be magic, too! Then I can roll over and turn into a buffalo and be big and strong—I don't want to go to sleep, I want to see her now!"

"No, Joe," Daddy said. "It's dark. The calf is asleep, like all little ones should be. We aren't here to touch, either. But we will go see her tomorrow."

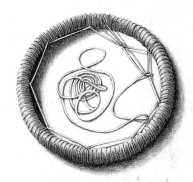

Sarah secretly wished the same thing: to touch magic. Although she knew the baby buffalo was not for petting, it was fun to pretend how its touch might let her do things she normally couldn't. Changing shapes wouldn't be too handy at school, but being able to hear and answer dreams or to save people in trouble—those were powers she thought anyone would like to have!

So, Sarah drifted off to sleep.

Daddy was snoring and Mama was sound asleep when suddenly Sarah woke up, startled. Something was wrong.

Joe was gone.

She jerked on her shoes and hurried to look for him. At the edge of the campground, a trail led up to the farm. It wasn't hard to figure out which way Joe had gone.

Sarah ran.

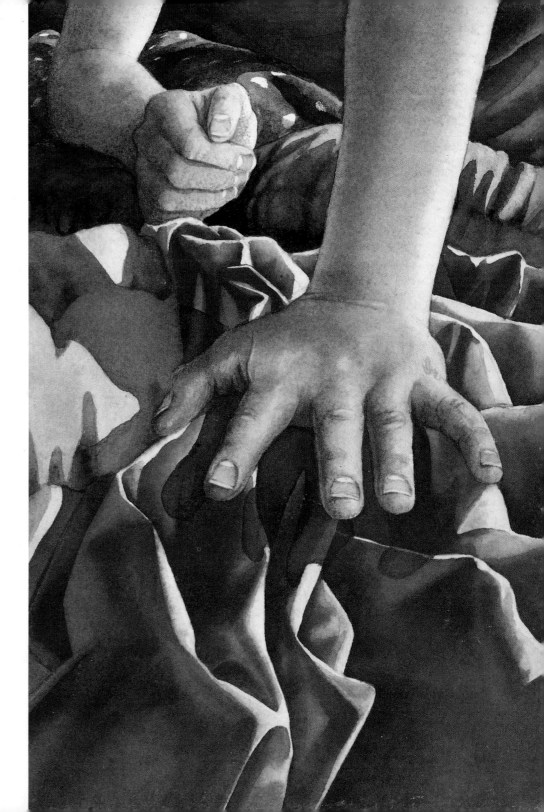

She spied Joe as he neared the barnyard. She hissed, "Joe! Get back here!" but he climbed right over the fence. Sarah got close enough to hear him breathe the word *magic* as he bounced toward the open barn door. She didn't think he saw the towering form in the shadows. Joe hadn't noticed the giant shape of a mother buffalo.

A thunderous bellow brought Joe up short. Joe froze in the middle of the corral, like a possum before headlights. Sarah scrambled over the fence. The angry mother buffalo stalked into the moonlight, eyeing Joe. She stopped, then began to snort and paw the ground. Her huge head swung back and forth, horns glinting.

"No! Stop!" Sarah cried.

The animal looked at her.

Sarah began to edge toward Joe.

"Stay still, Joey. She might charge."

She reached out and pulled Joe behind her. She could feel him shaking.

His breath came in pants, hot against her back. He seemed so small behind her.

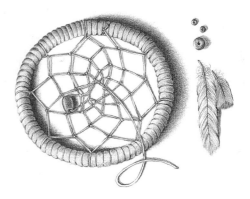

Suddenly, Sarah felt an odd strength fill her. Her hand rose. Although frightened, her voice was steady.

"Mama buffalo . . ." The huge animal paused.

The children took one step back.

"Please, don't hurt Joey. He's only a baby." Was she listening?

"He's only a calf."

Another step back.

"Please . . . let us go."

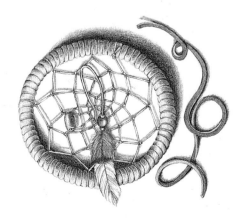

The mother buffalo stared as the children inched backward until they bumped the fence.

Sarah started to turn and follow Joe over the fence, but something coming from the barn door caught her eye.

The mother buffalo stood still as her white calf stepped into the moonlight and walked up to the girl. Slowly, Sarah stretched out her hand. An eager, damp nose nuzzled her palm. Moist warm breath flowed between her fingers. In the crisp night air, she could smell the mixture of straw and earth and warm, shaggy animal.

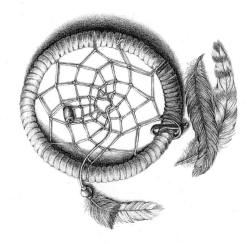

In a moment of forever, Sarah held magic.

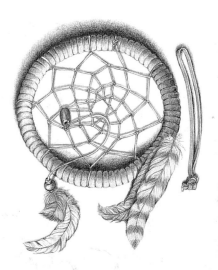

The spell was broken when the calf playfully shook her head, then trotted back to her mother.

"Thank you," Sarah whispered.

Suddenly, an angry voice erupted, "Good gosh a'mighty! What are you kids doing there?"

As the rancher loomed over them, voices came from everywhere.

"There they are!"

"Joe! Sarah! Oh, no!"

"Kids! What on earth . . . ?"

Sarah climbed out of the corral. Joe started crying as Mama and Daddy ran up, followed by several campers. Everyone had flashlights and scared faces. Sarah herself fought tears, as her parents kept switching from loud, angry words to frantic hugs. Only when Joe sobbed and suddenly flung himself into Sarah's arms did the adults calm down.

Daddy shook his head. "Sarah, I don't know what to say. You should never have followed Joe alone! But, then, you sure were brave."

People began to leave. Daddy apologized to the rancher and picked up Joe. The family walked quietly back to camp, until Mama broke the silence and said, "Sarah, you two scared me to death! We're so lucky nothing awful happened."

"I know. I'm really sorry." Then Sarah added, "But you know, Mama, both the mother buffalo and I were protecting someone we loved. I think she knew it."

"Maybe so, Sarah. She sure trusted you with her baby."

Then, Mama slowly smiled. "Like Joe said, you touched magic. Are you still our Sarah, or are you different now?"

Sarah grinned. "I'm still only me. I don't think I can do anything special, even though I touched a white buffalo. Now, that felt like magic."

Daddy said, "And you did do something special tonight, Daughter. You helped Joey."

"Daddy," Sarah said. "Maybe magic doesn't make you do something special. Maybe you do something special, and it makes magic."

Back at the camp, Sarah pulled the eagle feather from her pillowcase. She took her dreamcatcher down. As Sarah tied on the feather, her parents looked at each other in surprise.

"Weren't you going to give the feather to the white buffalo?" asked Mama.

Sarah nodded. "I still am."

Daddy knew at once what Sarah had in mind. His voice was warm. "Not only your strength, but your dreams. Your dreamcatcher is a fine gift, Daughter."

She stood and took his hand. Together, they walked back to the gift tree. They hung the dreamcatcher from just the right branch.

The dreams flowed that night, out of hearts, past the trees, across the hills, and floated through one certain dreamcatcher hanging from a gift tree, on into a nearby barn, where a small buffalo slept.

There, dreams became sweet grass, and open fields, and sunshine, and a little girl, playing with a woolly white friend.

THE LEGEND OF WHITE BUFFALO CALF WOMAN

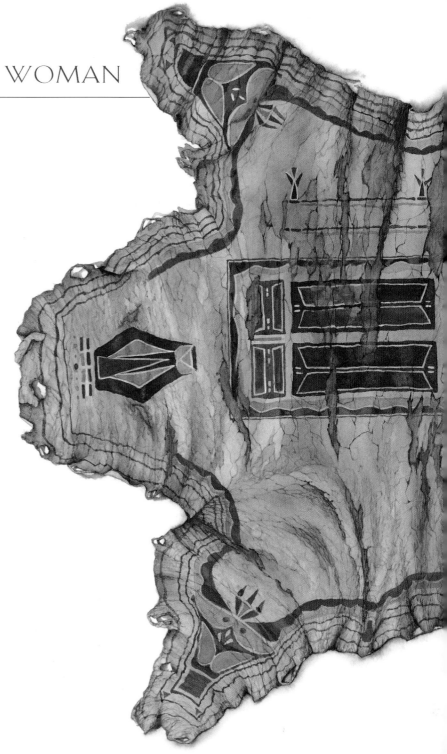

As two braves hunted the plains for game to save their starving tribe, they were amazed to see a beautiful woman approach them. She was dressed in white buckskin and walked without her moccasins touching the ground. One brave wanted her for his own. His friend disagreed. He warned that she could be a spirit. He said she should be treated with respect. But the other youth did not listen, and ran forward to capture her.

Suddenly, a dark cloud surrounded him. Thunder boomed, and lightning cracked the sky. When the cloud disappeared, only a pile of his bones remained at the woman's feet. The remaining brave stood and shook with terror. He pledged to honor this spirit and her wishes.

She told him to return to his lodge and make it ready for her. She said she would bring a gift for his people.

He returned to his tribe and they prepared for her. The spirit entered the camp and was seated in a place of honor. She produced a pipe and explained, "The length of this pipe is made of the plants that nourish you. It is to remind you of nature's many gifts. The bowl of the pipe is of red clay, a symbol of your flesh and bone. The smoke of the pipe is the breath of *Wakan*

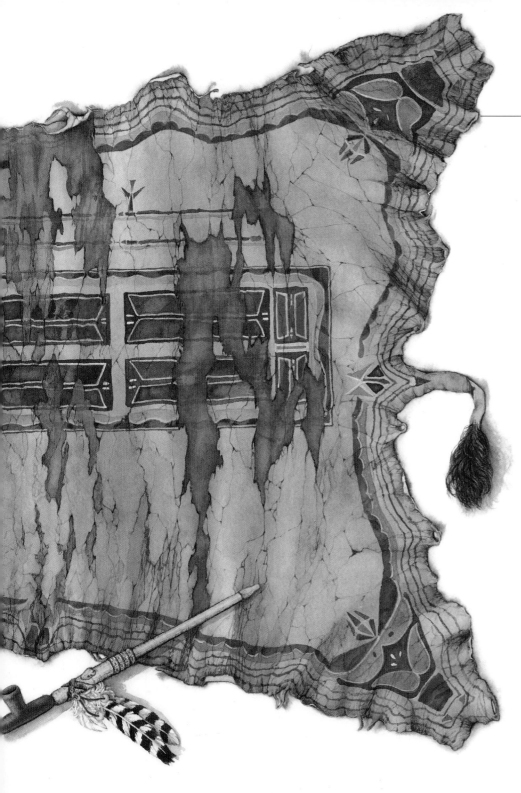

Tanka, the Great Spirit. This smoke will carry your dreams and needs up to the heavens, where I will hear and answer them."

She then showed them how to use and light the pipe—the peacemaker—for their ceremonies. She taught the people how to make fire, and blessed them with corn and pemmican. She gave them prayers of thanks to offer to *Wakan Tanka,* to the earth, and to the four winds from which all good things come.

She rose and walked into the sunset. When she reached the horizon, the people watched as she rolled on the ground and stood as a black buffalo. She rolled again, and was brown; a third time, she was red. The fourth time she rolled on the ground, the animal that stood was a white buffalo. Then she was gone.

They smoked the pipe that night; they sent her their dreams. The next morning, the tribe awoke to find a herd of buffalo had surrounded them during the night.

They were never hungry or cold again.

The dreamcatcher was invented by Native Americans long ago, to hang above their babies. Originally they were made of grapevines woven into circles no larger than your palm; now they come in all shapes and sizes. As the dreamcatcher idea has grown, so has the legend.

It is said that Grandmother Spider has woven a web inside this circle that hangs above a sleeper. At night, when dreams travel, the bad dreams are caught in her web and burn off when touched by the morning sun. But the good dreams slip through the center of the dreamcatcher, float off the feather at the end of the string, and live on in the heart of the dreamer. To draw in a favorite dream, tie to your dreamcatcher a keepsake of a favorite memory. Think about it just before you close your eyes, and . . . sweet dreams!

You will need:

a 6" metal hoop

10' of 1/4" rawhide
(chose a color)

15" of 1/4" rawhide
(same color)

3' of 1/4" rawhide
(a second color)

12' of waxed thread

beads with 1/8" centers

feathers

glue

favorite mementos

Before starting to weave, glue one end of the long rawhide to the hoop, and wrap it around the hoop until the hoop is covered. Tuck the end under the first loop and knot it.

1. To begin the web, turn the hoop so the knot is at 3:00 (you'll cover the knot later with the other rawhide). Tie the waxed thread to the hoop, and gently pull it toward the inside. Loop it under the hoop, back over the hoop, and under itself.

2. Keeping the thread loose, wind it under the hoop to the outside, over the hoop to the inside, and under itself. Make eight loops the same distance apart.

3. Tighten the thread at each loop until firm but not taut. Tie it off in a knot 1" from the first loop.

4. To begin the second row, make a loop in the center of the first row. Again, the pattern is under-to-back, over, then thread under itself.

5. Tighten the thread and even out the weave.

6. Begin the third row. At some point in this row, add a favorite bead; this is Grandmother Spider, the weaver of the dreamcatcher.

7. Weave more rows, but leave a center space big enough for one finger to pass through. Tie off with a knot.

8. Trim the thread to hang 4–5" below the dreamcatcher. Thread a few beads on it and tie one or two feathers to the end.

9. Wrap the other colored rawhide around the hoop over the original rawhide

knot, and tuck it under.

10. Put a dot of glue on the feather tips and slip them under the new rawhide band.

11. Fold the 15" rawhide in half and knot the ends around the hoop. Then wrap the loop over the first knot of the waxed thread to form a hanger.

12. Hang the dreamcatcher from its loop above your bed. As time goes on, add favorite letters, ribbons, charms,

This is for Betty and Otto Doner,
my parents.
My dreamcatchers.

Library of Congress Cataloging-in-Publication Data

Doner, Kim, 1955–
    Buffalo dreams / written and illustrated by Kim Doner.
       p.   cm.
    Summary: Having traveled with her family to see a newly born white buffalo and give her gifts, Sarah Bearpaw experiences a magic moment with the special calf. Includes a legend of the white buffalo and instructions for making a dreamcatcher.
       ISBN 1-55868-475-1 (hardcover : alk. paper)
       ISBN 1-55868-476-X (pbk. : alk. paper)
    1. Indians of North America—Juvenile fiction.   [1. Indians of North America—Fiction.   2. Bison—Fiction.]   I. Title.
PZ7.D71645Bu   1999   99-22577
[Fic]—dc21   CIP

WestWinds Press™
An imprint of Graphic Arts Center Publishing Company
P.O. Box 10306, Portland, Oregon 97296-0306, 503-226-2402
www.gacpc.com

President: Charles M. Hopkins
Editorial Staff: Douglas A. Pfeiffer, Ellen Harkins Wheat, Timothy W. Frew,
    Jean Andrews, Alicia I. Paulson, Deborah J. Loop,
    Joanna M. Goebel
Production Staff: Richard L. Owsiany, Susan Dupere
Designer: Elizabeth Watson

Printed in Singapore

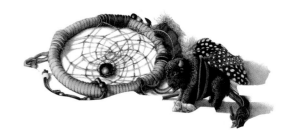